Interviewing for Information

by Stuart Schwartz and Craig Conley

Consultant:
Karen Wagner
Manager
Mankato WorkForce Center

CAPSTONE
HIGH/LOW BOOKS
an imprint of Capstone Press
Mankato, Minnesota

Capstone High/Low Books are published by Capstone Press
818 North Willow Street, Mankato, Minnesota 56001
http://www.capstone-press.com

Printed in the United States of America.

Library of Congress Cataloging-in-Publication Data

Schwartz, Stuart, 1945-

Interviewing for information/by Stuart Schwartz and Craig Conley.

p. cm.—(Looking at work)

Includes bibliographical references and index.

Summary: Describes techniques necessary for conducting interviews in order to learn more about different career fields and for evaluating the information received.

ISBN 0-7368-0179-0

1. Employment interviewing—Juvenile literature. 2. Employee selection—Juvenile literature. 3. Career development—Juvenile literature. [1. Job hunting. 2. Vocational guidance.] I. Conley, Craig, 1965-. II. Title. III. Series: Schwartz, Stuart, 1945- Looking at work.

HF5549.5.I6S364 1999

650.14—dc21 98-47356
CIP
AC

Editorial Credits

Carrie A. Braulick, editor; Steve Christensen, cover designer; Sheri Gosewisch and Kimberly Danger, photo researchers

Photo Credits

David F. Clobes, 16, 20
International Stock/Scott Barrow, cover
PhotoBank, Inc., 12; Photobank, Inc./Bill Lai, 10; John Connell, 14; J. Lafayette, 18
Shaffer Photography/James L. Shaffer, 4, 8, 22
Unicorn Stock Photos/Dennis MacDonald, 6
Visuals Unlimited/Jeff Greenberg, 24, 26

Table of Contents

Chapter 1

Informational Interviewing

Many people seek information about jobs and careers. A job is the work someone does to earn money. A career is the job area someone chooses to work in.

Students may need help deciding career paths. Recent graduates may need help finding jobs. Other people may want to change jobs or careers.

People can learn about jobs and careers by interviewing others. They can ask workers questions about their jobs or careers. This is called informational interviewing.

Informational interviewers can receive advice and information about jobs and careers. For example, they can learn what education is needed for certain jobs. They can find out what skills they need and how workers advance. Interviewers can learn how to improve their job searches.

Recent graduates may need help finding jobs.

CAREER
RESOURCE
CENTER

Chapter 2

Learning about Careers

Informational interviewers learn about careers before they set up interviews. They find information about careers that interest them. This research helps them get ready for their informational interviews.

Interviewers can go to employment agencies to learn about careers. Workers at these offices help people find jobs. They also offer career advice.

There are other ways to learn about careers. Public and school libraries collect information about many careers. School counselors and teachers often have career information.

Interviewers may talk to employers at career fairs. Employers hire and pay workers. Employers offer career advice and look for workers at career fairs.

Informational interviewers learn about careers that interest them.

Chapter 3

Finding a Contact

Informational interviewers must find contacts to interview. Contacts are people who work in certain careers. Interviewers receive information about jobs and careers from contacts.

Interviewers can find contacts through referrals. Referrals are names of people who might be contacts. Friends, family members, teachers, or co-workers can provide referrals. Contacts also may give interviewers referrals.

Interviewers can find contacts through other ways. They can use the Internet. The Internet is a system that allows people to share information with others through computers. Interviewers also can look in the Yellow Pages, newspaper articles, or business directories. The Yellow Pages is a section in a phone book that lists businesses by subject. Directories can provide lists of business names, addresses, and phone numbers.

Interviewers can look in the Yellow Pages to find contacts to interview.

Chapter 4

Setting up the Interview

Interviewers set up informational interviews through letters and phone calls. These letters and phone calls usually contain certain information.

Interviewers tell contacts who they are. They state their reasons for the interview requests. For example, interviewers might explain that they need help deciding which career paths to choose.

Interviewers ask for face-to-face interviews with their contacts. They usually set up 20- to 30-minute appointments. Some contacts are found through referrals. Interviewers tell contacts who gave the referrals.

Interviewers who send letters make follow-up phone calls. They call their contacts within two days to a week after the letters are sent. Interviewers arrange interview times when they make these phone calls. They ask contacts for phone interviews if the contacts cannot meet in person.

Many interviewers call contacts to set up informational interviews.

Chapter 5

Preparing for the Interview

Interviewers need to prepare before they interview their contacts. Interviewers who prepare are ready for their interviews.

Many interviewers make lists of questions they want to ask contacts. Interviewers should take their lists with them to interviews.

Interviewers may practice before their interviews. Many interviewers try to improve their communication skills. They practice asking questions with friends or relatives. They also practice listening. Listening closely helps interviewers understand the information they receive.

Interviewers wear proper clothes to informational interviews. Their clothes should be neat and businesslike.

Interviewers try to arrive 10 or 15 minutes before their appointments. Good interviewers are never late for interviews.

Interviewers practice asking questions with friends or relatives.

Chapter 6

Direct Questions

Interviewers ask direct questions. These questions usually have short, simple answers. Interviewers use direct questions to receive information quickly.

Interviewers can ask many direct questions. For example, they may ask about their contacts' job duties. They may ask what type of education is required for their contacts' careers. They may ask how much money people beginning in these careers earn. Interviewers may ask contacts if their career areas are growing.

Interviewers make sure to ask contacts for referrals. Interviewers should talk to as many contacts as possible. Each contact has different experiences, knowledge, and opinions. Interviewers can make better decisions if they have information and opinions from many people.

Interviewers ask contacts direct questions to receive information quickly.

Chapter 7

Open-Ended Questions

Interviewers also ask open-ended questions. These questions usually do not have short, simple answers.

Open-ended questions can start conversations between interviewers and contacts. Interviewers and contacts talk to each other about different career subjects. Many contacts share their opinions and ideas with interviewers. Open-ended questions help many interviewers gather a great deal of information.

Interviewers can ask many kinds of open-ended questions. For example, interviewers can ask what contacts like or dislike about their jobs. Interviewers can ask contacts how they feel about important areas in their careers. Interviewers can ask contacts if they would like to make changes in their careers.

Open-ended questions can start conversations between interviewers and contacts.

Chapter 8

During the Interview

Interviewers should know how to conduct their interviews. They want to gather as much information as possible. They also want contacts to form good opinions of them.

Interviewers introduce themselves when they meet their contacts. Interviewers tell contacts who they are. Interviewers shake hands with their contacts before their interviews.

Interviewers make sure they understand their contacts' answers. They may need to ask their contacts to explain some answers. Interviewers also may need to explain questions the contacts do not understand.

Many interviewers bring note pads and pens or pencils to their interviews. They write down information they want to remember.

Interviewers thank contacts for their help at the end of interviews. They shake hands with their contacts before they leave.

Interviewers shake hands with contacts before and after their interviews.

Chapter 9

Following Up

Interviewers follow up after their interviews. They send contacts thank-you letters. They also may keep in touch with their contacts.

Thank-you letters include certain information. Interviewers thank contacts for their time and effort. They write about information they learned at interviews. Interviewers also thank contacts for any referrals they provided. Interviewers make sure to include their names, addresses, and phone numbers in thank-you letters. Contacts may want to locate interviewers in the future.

Some interviewers keep in touch with their contacts. For example, interviewers can tell contacts about advances they make in their career searches.

Many interviewers find it helpful to keep in touch with contacts. For example, contacts may remember these interviewers if there are job openings at their companies.

Interviewers send their contacts thank-you letters after interviews.

IndyNet
"Your Internet Gateway"
The fastest, most reliable Internet connection available!
IndyNet
"Your Internet Gateway"
Superior Connectivity:
• Multiple T1s
• Redundant Paths
• 100% Fiber-Optic

Chapter 10

Internet Communication

The Internet can be helpful to interviewers. It allows interviewers to communicate with contacts through computers.

Interviewers may use e-mail to send messages to contacts on the Internet. E-mail is a short word for electronic mail. Many interviewers use e-mail when face-to-face interviews are not possible.

Interviewers need to know their contacts' e-mail addresses in order to send messages to them. Interviewers may find contacts' e-mail addresses in directories.

Some interviewers communicate with contacts in Internet chat rooms. Interviewers and contacts write messages to each other at the same time in chat rooms. Chat rooms are sorted into certain subjects. For example, there are chat rooms about movies and books. Interviewers can find chat rooms about careers.

Interviewers can use the Internet to communicate with contacts.

Chapter 11

Evaluating the Information

Interviewers must evaluate the information they receive from interviews. They review the information contacts gave them. They consider how this information meets their needs.

Interviewers think about their contacts' career areas. Interviewers may consider how they can advance in these careers. They may think about the education or training these careers require. Interviewers may want to find more information. For example, interviewers may want to research new careers they learned about at interviews.

Interviewers make decisions after they evaluate the information. They may find that they do not want to work in certain careers. They also may decide that some careers are perfect for them.

Interviewers consider how the information they learned from interviews meets their needs.

Campbell's
Cream of Broccoli
SOUP

Chapter 12

Improving a Job Search

Interviews can help people improve their job searches. Interviewers may even learn about job openings through their contacts.

Some interviewers discover ways to improve their resumés. A resumé is a written summary of a person's experience, job skills, and education. Resumés help people get jobs.

Interviewers learn how to write their resumés to fit certain jobs. For example, some jobs require good social skills. Interviewers seeking these jobs can include volunteer work on their resumés. Volunteers work for free. They often are helpful and friendly to others.

Informational interviews also are good practice for job interviews. People who have done informational interviews may feel more comfortable talking to employers. Informational interviews are good career planning and job search tools. They help interviewers find rewarding, satisfying careers.

Interviewers can include volunteer work on their resumés to show certain skills.

Words to Know

contact (KON-takt)—a person who works in a certain career; interviewers receive information about jobs and careers from contacts.

direct question (duh-REKT KWESS-chuhn)—a simple, clear question interviewers ask to receive information quickly

Internet (IN-tur-net)—a system that allows people to share information with others through computers; interviewers may use e-mail on the Internet to send messages to contacts.

open-ended question (OH-puhn-EN-ded KWESS-chuhn)—a question that allows contacts to give their opinions and ideas

referral (ri-FUR-uhl)—a name of a person who might be a contact to interview

resumé (RE-zuh-may)—a written summary of a person's experience, job skills, and education

To Learn More

Hirsch, Arlene S. and Tony Lee. *Interviewing.* National Business Employment Weekly. New York: John Wiley & Sons, 1996.

McFarland, Rhoda. *The World of Work.* Lifeskills Library. New York: Rosen Publishing Group, 1993.

Schwartz, Stuart and Craig Conley. *Finding Work.* Looking at Work. Mankato, Minn.: Capstone High/Low Books, 1998.

Stoodley, Martha. *Information Interviewing: How to Tap Your Hidden Job Market.* Chicago: J. G. Ferguson Publishing, 1997.

Useful Addresses

Human Resources Development Canada
140 Promenade du Portage, Phase IV
Hull, QC K1A OJ9
Canada

National Career Development Association
4700 Reed Road, Suite M
Columbus, OH 43220

U.S. Department of Labor
Office of Public Affairs
200 Constitution Avenue NW
Room S-1032
Washington, DC 20210

Internet Sites

America's Career InfoNet

http://www.acinet.org/acinet/resource

Canada WorkInfoNet

http://www.workinfonet.ca/cwn

JobTrak

http://www.jobtrak.com

UWEC Career Services

http://www.uwec.edu/admin/career/faqs

Index